SCREAM STREET™

A SNEER DEATH EXPERIENCE

The fiendish fun continues at

www.screamstreet.com

For Sam Donbavand

First published 2016 by Walker Books Ltd
87 Vauxhall Walk, London SE11 5HJ

2 4 6 8 10 9 7 5 3 1

© 2016 Coolabi Productions Limited
Based on the Scream Street series of books by Tommy Donbavand

Based on the scripts "Banished!" and "Light Fingers"
by Mark Huckerby and Nick Ostler.

This book has been typeset in Bembo Educational

Printed and bound in Great Britain by Clays Ltd, St Ives plc

British Library Cataloguing in Publication Data: a catalogue record for this book is available from the British Library

ISBN 978-1-4063-6785-0
www.walker.co.uk

A SNEER DEATH
EXPERIENCE

Tommy Donbavand

WALKER
ENTERTAINMENT

LUKE WATSON

With a troublesome taste for adventure, Luke is much like any other teenage boy – oh, except for the fact that he's also a werewolf. If he gets upset, stay well clear of him!

CLEO FARR

Cleo is a feisty teen mummy who's been in Scream Street for centuries. She's used that time to become an expert at martial arts, which comes in handy rather often.

RESUS NEGATIVE

Resus is the sarcastic son of two vampires. But he didn't get the vampire gene himself, so there's no drinking blood or turning into a bat for him – much to his disappointment.

MAYOR SNEER

Scream Street's mayor, Sir Otto Sneer, is a "normal" person. But his scheming plans for the community are more monstrous than any of the residents!

DIXON

Sneer's dim-witted trainee has the remarkable ability to shift into any person, creature or object. The only clue that it's him is a signature green stripe.

NILES FARR

Although he loves his daughter, Cleo, very much, Niles is a brainless mummy – literally!

SCREAM STREET™

1. THE GHOST TRAIN
2. HAUNTED HOUSE
3. EEFA'S EMPORIUM
4. SNEER HALL

WHERE BEING A FREAK IS TOTALLY NORMAL...

5 CLEO'S HOUSE

6 THE GRAVEYARD

7 RESUS'S AND LUKE'S HOUSES

CONTENTS

BANISHED!

LIGHT FINGERS

Chapter One
THE SAFE ROOM

The zombie shuffled awkwardly along the street in the rain, one leg dragging behind as though it didn't want to go along with whatever depraved plan the undead creature had in mind. Still, the twisted limb kept pace.

Step, drag… Step, drag… Step, drag…

As the deluge of rain lashed down onto the monster's greasy, matted hair, an entire family of cockroaches washed free from the disgusting locks and down the zombie's pockmarked face.

13

The beast stuck out its purple, bloated tongue to catch the unexpected treats, then crunched down on them, feeling them burst open. It continued to lurch onwards.

Striving to see through the torrential rain, the zombie's milky, leaking eyeballs eventually focused on a figure up ahead: a young boy, sitting innocently next to the open window of his living room, just three houses down. The creature twisted its mouth into what might have been a smile, then picked up speed.

The boy didn't see or hear the zombie as it limped closer. He was facing away from his stalker, lost in the antics of a popular presenter on the screen in front of him. The monster reached out and grabbed his shoulder with long-nailed fingers, pus oozing freely from the open sores that covered the gripping hand.

"Doug!" cried Luke Watson, spinning round to face his zombie friend. "How's it going?"

"Totally righteous, little dude!" beamed the creature, flicking his limp, wet hair away from his eyes. "I'm just out for my morning constitutional."

Luke's eyes flicked up to the churning grey clouds that filled the sky. "Not ideal weather for

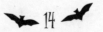

it," he said. "Do you want to come in, out of the rain?"

"Thanks, but no thanks, old pal," Doug replied. "Can't beat a good downpour to wash the bed bugs out of your brain. I hope it lasts."

"Let's find out," said Luke, snatching up a wand and flicking it in front of the magic mirror on the wall. The game show he had been watching – called *The Price is Fright* – disappeared, and a zombie weather reporter appeared in its place.

"Hey, that's Mitch Flesh!" cried Doug. "My favourite!"

The pair watched as the weatherman finished his report: "...the stormy conditions are set to continue, with intermittent hail, thunder and lightning. In summary, it's another beautiful day in Scream Street!"

"Hail?" mused Doug, peering upwards. "I haven't noticed any—"

Before the zombie could finish his sentence, huge hailstones the size of potatoes began to clatter down from the sky. Doug yelped as the massive balls of ice pummelled him to the ground.

"Are you OK?" asked Luke, once the shower had subsided and it was safe to stick his head out

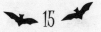

of the window again.

"Never better, dude," groaned the zombie, struggling to lift his battered body out of the mud. "At least it wasn't the—"

Crrrraaassshhh!

An electric blue bolt of lightning rocketed from the churning clouds and smashed straight into Doug's chest. Luke fell back off the sofa, his vision burning from the flash of light. He scrambled back up, rubbing his eyes, and was amazed to find Doug not only upright, but also dancing in the rainstorm.

"Wahey!" cackled the cavorting corpse. "Now *that's* got the old engine running!" The zombie paused to lick his lips. "I think I might go find a party that's in need of some Doug."

Luke shook his head as Doug leapt over the garden fence and hurried away. Then he turned his attention back to the magic mirror, just as the weather zombie grabbed a handful of his own hair and ripped off his head. Tossing the bonce aside, the body reached beneath the newsdesk for a replacement – this one female – and stuck it onto the exposed piece of spine jutting out between its shoulders.

"Thanks, Mitch," said the newly noggined

newscaster. "Coming up: Crazed resident banished to the Underlands."

Luke leaned towards the screen as the image changed to footage of yet another zombie, this one being dragged towards a fiery portal by NoName, the mayor of Scream Street's huge hired henchman.

"No!" the crazed creature yelled. "I'll be good! I promise!"

NoName hesitated at the edge of the portal. The monstrous minder didn't have a face, just an expanse of smooth skin, so it was impossible to tell quite what he was thinking. Luke imagined he was considering giving the convicted criminal a second chance. The Underlands were the dreaded land beneath Scream Street, where monsters were sent when they turned on their neighbours.

Suddenly, the zombie lunged for NoName's leg, teeth bared. But the bulging bodyguard was too quick. Shoving two massive fingers up the zombie's nostrils, he flicked the miscreant, still screaming for mercy, through the portal of fire and down into the terrifying world below.

Luke shuddered as the picture switched back to Anna Gored, the newsreader.

"Lastly," she said with a twisted smile, "a

reminder for all residents that there will be a special announcement at today's town meeting. Attendance at the meeting is, as ever, compulsory. Absentees will be strung up in the town square by their—"

"Luke!" cried a voice from upstairs.

Luke grabbed the wand and turned off the magic mirror. "Yes, Mum?"

"Time for the safe-room drill!"

"Oh, no," said Luke to himself as he headed for the stairs. "Not this again."

Ever since moving to Scream Street, Luke's parents had been searching for a way to keep themselves safe whenever their son transformed into his werewolf. They'd tried locking him inside a cage once, but quickly discovered that the wolf was strong enough to bend the bars.

They'd also tried chains, only to find that the lengths of metal gave Luke's werewolf a handy weapon to wield in addition to its teeth and claws.

So, Mike Watson had set about building a safe room – a sealed vault that he and his wife, Sue, could lock themselves into whenever Luke "went a bit wolfy". There had, however, been teething problems, and Mike and Sue had decided to initiate a series of tests whenever the safe room was upgraded.

Luke found his dad at the top of the stairs, tongue sticking out of his mouth as he concentrated on fitting an elaborate new lock to the inside of the safe-room door.

"Ready, dear?" asked Sue, as Luke reached the landing.

"Ready as I'll ever be!" Luke said, forcing a smile.

"Right!" said Mike, tucking the screwdriver into his pocket. "Let's see how long it takes your mother and me to lock ourselves inside my new and improved safe room."

Nobody moved.

"What are you waiting for?" Luke asked.

"Motivation!" cried Mike. "The room might be ready to keep us safe from your wolf's pointy bits – but I'm not really feeling the fear, if you get my meaning."

Luke rolled his eyes. In their old life, Mike had been a long-standing member of the local amateur dramatic society, a passion he'd not yet found an outlet for in Scream Street.

"OK," Luke sighed. He held up his hands to

look like paws. "Roar."

"No, no, no!" exclaimed Mike. "Where's the terror? Where's the anger? Where's the wolf?"

"What, you actually want me to transform?" Luke asked.

"Oh good gracious no!" said his father quickly. "I just want you to give your performance a little more ... bite, shall we say. Now, once more, with feeling."

This time, Luke closed his eyes and dug down, deep inside himself. He pictured the first time he had ever transformed in public, when he had been trying to protect an innocent classmate from a beating by a school bully. He remembered how it had felt when the bully turned on him instead. How each blow had pushed him closer and closer to setting the werewolf free...

"Rrrooooaaaarrrrrr!"

Mike squealed in terror as Luke raced towards him. He grabbed his wife's hand, pulled her inside the safe room, and slammed the door. Instantly, the new lock activated, metal scraping against metal as the heavy bolts locked into place.

Bang! Clunk! Thump!

"There!" said Mike, when he could catch his

breath. "Perfect!"

"Ahem."

Mike shrieked and jumped into his wife's arms. Luke was standing inside the safe room with them. "I'm pretty sure you're not supposed to let the werewolf in here with you," he said with a grin.

Sue gently lowered her husband to the ground. "I guess we need to be a little quicker," she said, checking her watch. "But there's no time for a rerun now. We don't want to be late for the town meeting."

Retracting the bolts, she flung the door open and led her still-trembling husband down the stairs. Luke made to follow, until his foot clanked against something on the ground. The new handle had fallen off the back of the door.

"Hey, Dad!" he called, bending to pick it up. "You didn't screw this in prop—"

Click!

The reinforced door to the safe room swung shut. Luke gave it a push. It was locked tight.

"Seriously?" he groaned.

THE MEETING

Mike and Sue Watson joined the throng of residents hurrying towards the gates of Sneer Hall, the stately residence of Scream Street's mayor, Sir Otto Sneer. They joined vampires, bog monsters, skeletons, zombies and others, all eager to avoid being chastised for arriving late at the mandatory meeting.

"Come on, Luke! Keep up!" called Sue over her shoulder, unaware that her son was still at home, trying to pick the lock on the safe-room door with a hastily transformed werewolf claw.

Security was tight, and the Watsons soon found themselves herded past the latest safeguards installed by the perpetually paranoid Otto: cameras fitted with human eyeballs, walls topped with barbed wire, and Dixon – the mayor's green-haired, shape-shifting assistant – with his clipboard and broken pencil.

Otto Sneer was, in his own words, "a normal", and he usually avoided contact with "the freaks" (again, his words) who populated the houses in his community. Unless, of course, he had an important announcement to make, in which case he wanted everyone in attendance. This looked to be one of those occasions.

An uneasy hush fell over the residents as everyone gathered inside Sneer Hall's sumptuous banqueting room. The dining table and chairs had been pushed aside to create space for a vast magic mirror in a gold frame, and something hidden beneath a sheet.

Young vampire Resus Negative spotted his friend, Cleo Farr, near the front of the crowd and, holding his slobbering giant leech, Lulu, pushed his way through to her.

"Any idea what this is all about?" he asked the Egyptian mummy as he arrived.

"No," hissed Cleo. "But if we're here to listen to someone from the Mayor Sir Otto Sneer Fan Club again, I'm leaving."

"I don't mind those meetings," Resus admitted, perching Lulu on his shoulder. "It was the movie I couldn't take: *Mayor Sir Otto Sneer: The Man, the Mystery*. That's four hours of my life I'm never getting back."

Suddenly, a spotlight hit a small podium in front of the magic mirror, and two goblins were lowered from the ceiling on lengths of rope. They both spun round to point their bottoms towards the assembled tenants, then farted a fanfare.

NoName, the mayor's massive manservant, held up a hand-painted sign that read "APPLAUSE" and Otto Sneer jogged out of a nearby door to hop up onto the podium and wave.

No one clapped.

"Residents of Scream Street!" the mayor bellowed. "As much as you like coming to these meetings to listen to me talk..."

A rumble of muttered disagreement swept

across the room, but Otto continued. "Today, you will be hearing from an even greater man than me. Live from G.H.O.U.L. HQ, the President himself … Greystoke McDread!"

Behind Otto, the giant magic mirror flickered to life, revealing the beaming face of the leader of the secretive organization known as Government Housing of Unusual Lifeforms, or G.H.O.U.L.

The atmosphere in the room changed instantly. Here was the man responsible for allowing many of the residents to leave their lives of torture and torment at the hands of humans and relocate to the relative safety of Scream Street. Vampires had been saved from angry, pitchfork-wielding mobs. Witches had avoided an appointment with the hangman's noose. And several mummies had been saved from centuries of boredom trapped in tombs.

This time, there was a round of applause.

Greystoke McDread accepted the welcome with a slight bow of his head. "Ever since G.H.O.U.L. rescued you all from the horrors of the normal world and brought you here to Scream Street, I have only ever wanted to give you better lives."

Somewhere near the back of the room a mummy gave out a "whoop", a skeleton cheered and a pair of dismembered zombie arms applauded.

McDread bristled with pleasure. "So, I'm happy to announce the next phase in Scream Street's development."

The goblins pumped out another gaseous fanfare as Otto snatched the sheet away from a nearby table, revealing a model of a completely redesigned Scream Street. The residents gasped with excitement as they crowded around to view it.

"Look!" cried Resus's dad. "Blood-filled hot tubs!"

"Swimming pools!" gurgled Mr Crudley, the bog monster.

"Landscaped gardens!" exclaimed Sue.

At the front of the thrilled throng, Resus and Cleo exchanged a wide-eyed glance. "Home cinemas!" they shouted, giving each other a high-five.

Resus waited until Cleo had turned her attention back to the model before shaking the stinging pain out of his palm.

Greystoke McDread continued to beam down at them from the magic mirror. "Simply sign the consent forms," he announced, "and soon you will be living a life of luxury. Even those of you who aren't technically alive."

NoName began to hand out the consent forms, which everyone took and signed eagerly. They were all so busy chatting about their future opulence that they ignored Greystoke when he added, quietly and rapidly: "Your current homes will be destroyed, along with any possessions, loved ones or pets still inside. That's it. Bye-bye."

The image on the magic mirror hissed and faded, and Otto Sneer began to chuckle.

As the residents filed out of Sneer Hall, Resus and Cleo were happily discussing which movies they planned to watch first once their home cinemas had been installed.

"What about *Curse of the Mummy's Tomb*?" asked Resus.

Cleo scowled. "Are you serious?"

"Yeah, why not?"

"Because not all tombs have curses on them! It's stereotyping mummies! How would you like it if I made you sit through *Blood-Soaked Vampires 4*?"

Resus shrugged. "I'd probably love it."

"You would not!" Cleo scoffed. "You practically fainted when Luke fell off his skateboard and cut his knee last week — and that only bled a little bit."

Resus shuddered at the memory. "That was more than enough for me, thank you."

Cleo grinned. She knew that Resus, despite being born to vampire parents, was in fact a normal boy. He wore clip-on fangs, dyed his hair black, and steered clear of anything that involved real blood.

"Look," she said, pointing across the square. "Here comes old bleedy knees now."

Resus squinted to see Luke racing towards them. He had transformed his legs into those of his werewolf to gain extra speed.

"It's a good job I signed you in at the meeting or you'd be in major trouble," Resus said.

"Thanks!" gasped Luke, trying to catch his breath as his legs returned to normal. "What did I miss?"

"Oh, not much," said Cleo with a barely

disguised grin. "Just Greystoke McDread himself – unveiling the future of Scream Street!"

Luke's eyes grew wide. "What?"

"Swimming pools! Home cinemas!" enthused Resus. "You should have seen it!"

"Maybe I still can," said Luke, turning and running through the gates of Sneer Hall.

Back inside the banqueting room, Greystoke McDread was back on the giant magic mirror. Otto Sneer stood before it, rubbing his hands together.

"Well, I thought that went rather well!" he cackled.

"See?" said McDread. "I told you I could do it!"

"Yes, well done," said Otto. "But you can change back now, Dixon. The sight of that blowhard on the big screen for too long gives me the creeps."

"Aw," moaned McDread. "This body made me feel important!"

"You'll feel the back of my hand if you don't change right this minute!"

"Oh, all right," McDread grumbled, sweeping

a length of green hair from his eyes. The figure stepped off the screen and out from behind the vast mirror, where his skin began to ripple and change shape. Within a few seconds, the mayor's assistant stood in Greystoke McDread's place.

"Dixon!" cried a voice.

Otto spun to find Luke standing in the doorway. "How long have you been standing there, boy?" he spat. "How much have you seen?"

"Enough to know you're taking everyone in Scream Street for a ride!" said Luke angrily. "You promised everyone new homes!"

"And here they are," said Dixon, resting a hand on the table. "See..."

As Luke crossed the room to look at the model, Dixon pressed a little too hard and the entire table surface flipped over to reveal a second model underneath. This one had the grounds of Sneer Hall expanded to cover almost all of Scream Street. The new estate included a golf course, several swimming pools, an artificial ski slope and even a shopping mall called the Sneer Centre.

There was a tiny strip of land outside the fence filled with tents. Tents, Luke realized to his horror, where the rest of the residents would be living.

"Don't show him that!" bellowed Otto, scrabbling to grab the sheet from the floor and cover up the new model.

"So, that's your real plan?" asked Luke. "A nice big palace for *you* to live in and crummy tents for the rest of us? You just wait until I tell everyone!"

Luke turned to leave, but Otto snapped his fingers and NoName grabbed him by the shoulder.

"I don't think you'll be doing that, young man," snarled the mayor.

Luke struggled against NoName's grip. "Get off, you big ... whatever you are!"

Otto stepped up to Luke and smiled nastily. "Oh, dear," he said. "Getting a little hot under the collar, are we?"

Luke glared back at Otto as a familiar dark feeling began to sweep over his body. "You don't know the half of it!" he growled.

"Look out!" cried Dixon. "He's starting his werewolf transformation!" NoName let go of Luke and took a step backwards.

"Then we'd better let him cool off outside!" said Otto. He reached out and pulled a lever on the wall, opening up a trapdoor beneath Luke's feet. The werewolf tumbled down the hatch and out a hole in the outer wall. He landed in a large metal cage strapped to the side of the building.

Otto and Dixon watched as Luke's wolf gripped the metal bars with its huge paws and howled. The wolf strained, but the extra-thick metal bars didn't budge.

"Won't he just tell everyone about our plans when he changes back?" Dixon asked.

A smile snaked its way across Otto's face. "Yes, but we'll just have to make sure that no one listens."

Chapter Three
THE DESTRUCTION

Luke slowly opened his eyes. They hurt, along with every other part of his body. He was lying on a carpet, surrounded by splintered wood, broken bricks and clouds of dust.

Sunlight was streaming in through a hole in the roof. Bits of plaster fell from around the jagged gap, pattering against his face and ragged clothing.

With every muscle screaming, Luke pushed himself up and rested on his elbows. He was at home! The building around him — what was left of it — was 13 Scream Street. But that meant...

"Mum? Dad?"

There was a creaking sound, then a door fell off its hinges. Just inside the safe room crouched Mike and Sue Watson, hugging each other tightly.

The new handle was still lying on the floor next to the doorframe.

Luke clambered to his feet.

Mike shrank back. "Careful, Luke," he said. "You're still a bit ... you know ... grrr!"

"Huh?" Luke looked down at his feet to see that he still had werewolf paws, tipped with long talons. He closed his eyes for a moment, concentrated hard, and they began to shrink back into something more human.

He paused halfway up the stairs. "Did I do all this?" he breathed.

"Well..." began Sue.

Then Luke noticed a long scratch on her cheek.

"Mum!"

She raised her hand, covering the thin red line. "I'm all right," she said. "We both are, really."

"Then why aren't you coming out of the safe room?" Luke asked.

Slowly, cautiously, the Watsons edged nervously towards their son.

Part of the bannister collapsed.

"In a way, this is a good thing," said Sue, as cheerily as she could. "It just proves that we need to be able to get to the safe room a little quicker next time."

Luke's head was spinning, and he was having difficulty putting the day's events into any kind of sensible order.

He remembered meeting Resus and Cleo outside Sneer Hall, and their excitement at the new developments announced by Greystoke McDread. Luke had wanted to find out more, so he had hurried into the mayor's banqueting suite just in time to see Dixon shape-shift back to his usual body.

Dixon had been pretending to be the head of G.H.O.U.L.!

And Otto Sneer was planning—

"It's the mayor!" Luke cried, jumping to his feet. Mike and Sue took an involuntary step back. "He's planning to change Scream Street!"

35

"We know," said Mike. "We were at the meeting as well."

"No," said Luke. "You don't understand. The model you saw is not the *real* plan. Otto Sneer is—"

"Here at last!" cried a voice.

Luke turned to see the mayor pushing his way through the ruins at the front of the house. He reached a particularly stubborn section of what had been the living room wall, and paused long enough for NoName to stomp it into rubble.

"Oh my!" exclaimed Otto dramatically, as he took in the ruined surroundings. "The tragedy! The pain of it all!"

"Mr Mayor!" said Mike, scurrying down the stairs, squeezing up against the wall to get past Luke. "Sorry! It's not usually this messy."

"Oh, please, it's no trouble!" gushed Otto. "But tea would be nice, when you're ready."

"Of course!" said Mike, pushing through the broken door to the kitchen. He began to search through the debris for the kettle. "Tea, tea, tea..."

"I simply had to come the moment I heard the news," Otto continued. "Parents attacked in their own home, by their own son! Oh, it's just awful!"

Luke struggled to keep his temper; he couldn't risk transforming again now. "I only changed because of you," he said through gritted teeth. "You didn't want me telling anyone about your *real* plans for Scream Street. You're a danger—"

Otto abruptly wrapped his arms around Luke and hugged him tightly to his chest, muffling the rest of his words.

"Mffff-mff-mmmf-mmfff!"

"Oh, you poor, confused child!" Otto wailed. "I think if anyone's a danger, it's you, isn't it?"

Luke fought to free himself from the mayor's grip, but Otto leaned in and whispered in his ear. "If it weren't for you, *freak*, your parents could return to their old lives in the normal world. Just imagine how happy that would make them!"

Released from Otto's grasp, Luke looked back to where his mum was dabbing at the scratch on her cheek. Then he turned to the kitchen to see his dad boiling water in a battered saucepan.

Otto was right. This mess was all his fault, and it was only a matter of time before his werewolf transformations resulted in something a lot worse than a few broken doors and a scratched face.

 37

With a deep sigh, Luke turned and walked out of the house.

"Luke!" cried Sue, hurrying down the stairs. But before she could chase after her son, Otto stepped in her way with a long sheet of paper.

"Here's the bill for the repairs we'll need to make – before we knock the place down again, of course. Payment is due first thing tomorrow morning. Now, where's that cup of tea?"

"Coming!" called Mike, grabbing the one mug that hadn't been shattered into pieces. He lifted the saucepan from the stove and poured the hot water, which splashed to the floor around his feet.

"Oh, dear," he said, peering into the mug. "It's got no bottom!"

Luke trudged through the woods on the outskirts of Scream Street, his shoulders slumped and his eyes downcast. He tried to remember what life had been like before he and his parents moved to this wretched community.

He'd had friends at school. No one like Resus and Cleo, of course, but kids he'd been happy to hang around with in the playground at break times.

 38

He'd lived in a nice home, too. Nothing posh, and not very big, but enough for the three of them. They'd had a garden with a trampoline, and one summer his dad had built a barbecue out of old bricks. It wasn't entirely successful – the grill was on a slant, which meant the sausages all rolled down to one end – but it had been fun to cook outdoors in the summer with his family.

Then the wolf had come along and ruined everything.

Otto was right: Luke was a freak. Dangerous, too. And there was only one place where dangerous monsters should be.

He heard a snuffling sound behind and turned to see the furry front half of a dog trotting after him. The back end of the canine was nothing but skeleton.

"Go away, Dig!" Luke muttered. But the half-hound didn't want to go away. He continued following Luke as he made his way deeper and deeper into the woods.

Finally, Luke stopped and faced his companion. "Look, buddy, you can't come with me where I'm going. Nobody can." Then he set off again.

 39

Dig made one more attempt to follow but after a final, sharp "Dig, *no!*" the pooch's bony tail drooped, and he scampered off back in the direction of Scream Street.

By the time Dig reached the central square, residents were queuing to collect their shabby tents from NoName. All around, homes were being cordoned off, ready for demolition.

"Remember," Otto announced through a loudhailer. "These are only temporary. You'll all be in your new, luxury homes before you know it!"

He lowered the loudhailer and grinned at Dixon.

"Chumps!"

Dig raced past the queue in the square, heading straight for number 13 Scream Street. Inside, Resus and Cleo were rummaging through the rubble.

"Do you really think Luke did this?" asked Resus.

Cleo shrugged. "Maybe," she said. "It's possible."

"Then where is he?"

"I don't know," Cleo answered. "It's not like him just to take off like that."

Resus reached down to pick up a broken painting that had fallen from one of the walls. Just as his fingers touched the frame, Dig's head appeared through the middle of the torn canvas. The vampire squealed in fright and fell over.

"Dig!" he cried. "It's you!"

"Hey, look at this!" said Cleo, pulling back a length of ripped curtain. Embedded in the wall was a large, broken claw. "Ouch!" she said. "That must have hurt."

She gripped the claw with her fingers and pulled hard, just as Resus clambered to his feet behind her. The claw came free, Cleo's arm jolted back, and her elbow hit him square in the chest. Resus crashed to the floor with another squeal.

Dig was on him in seconds, licking at his face.

"Gerroff!" Resus yelled. "You'll have all my make up off!"

"Do you think this is one of Luke's?" Cleo asked, holding up the claw.

Resus took the talon and examined it. "Well, if it isn't, his pet hamster's grown a lot since I last saw it."

Dig trotted over for a look. He sniffed at the claw, then backed away, growling. The fur on the front part of his back stood on end.

"Great idea, Dig!" said Cleo, snatching the claw back from Resus. "Now, get a good whiff – and take us to Luke!"

Chapter Four
THE GATEKEEPER

Luke's vast werewolf paws hacked and slashed their way through the undergrowth, all ten of his razor-sharp claws slicing through branches as if they were made of paper.

He'd been walking for just over an hour, but it felt five times that long. The woodland here was dense and unkempt. Tree roots tripped him up, and long, drooping vines encircled his arms as he battled onwards.

It was almost as though the forest didn't want

him to go any further.

But Luke wasn't about to give up. He had made a decision, and he was going to stick to it, no matter how difficult. It would be better for everyone this way.

His cheeks scratched by thorny bushes and skin reddened by the sting of nettles, Luke continued to battle his way through the tangled mess of greenery until he stumbled out into an open clearing.

He paused to catch his breath, his werewolf paws shrinking. The air around him was stale – and warm, as though someone had lit a bonfire nearby.

That could only mean one thing...

Yes! There it was, on the opposite side of the clearing, nestled between the giant roots of a gnarled, old tree. The fiery entrance to the Underlands.

Luke took a step forward, the heat from the burning portal already beginning to singe the hair on his arms. Through the haze, he could just make out the white-hot centre of the gateway. The hole through which there would be no coming back. The Underlands were known for their black scorched earth, churning purple skies, desolation for mile after mile, and some of the nastiest, most perilous creatures ever known to civilization. From terrible trolls to uncontrollable unicorns, poisonous pixies to leering leprechauns, the worst of the worst inhabited the Underlands.

That was why Luke had to go there now, before he seriously hurt someone he loved. Or worse.

Taking a deep breath, Luke strode towards the burning opening.

"No turning back now…"

Suddenly, a piece of bark in the tree above the portal lifted, and an eyeball swivelled round to look at him. Luke jumped back in alarm.

"Who dares to approach the gateway to the Underlands?" boomed a voice.

Luke stared up at the tree in shock. There were two eyes now. A short branch for a nose, and a wide split in the bark that looked exactly like a mouth.

"Excuse me?" said Luke. "Did you just … talk?"

"Of course I did," said the tree. "Who else do you think it was?"

Luke glanced around. He was alone in the clearing.

 45

"It's just that ... I've never heard a tree talk before."

"And?"

Luke shrugged. "I dunno. I suppose I expected your voice to sound a bit more ... wooden."

"Wooden?" roared the tree.

"Yes," Luke admitted. "Well, you are a tree."

"I am the Gatekeeper!"

"Right," said Luke. "Hello."

"Now, about this 'wooden' business..."

"That's my point," said Luke hurriedly. "You don't sound wooden at all. You've got a great voice."

"Oh," bellowed the tree. "Thank you."

"You're welcome," said Luke. 'Well, I can't hang around all day..."

"How would you describe it?"

Luke blinked. "Describe what?"

"My voice!" thundered the tree. "Describe it to me."

"Er ... it's very ... nice," said Luke.

"Nice?" the Gatekeeper rumbled. "*Nice?*"

"Yes, what's wrong with that?"

"Ladybirds are *nice*!" the tree pointed out. "The first flowers in spring are *nice*."

"Oh, all right," said Luke, thinking. "Magnificent, then. Your voice is magnificent!"

"You really think so?"

"I do," said Luke. "Now, if you will excuse me..."

"Who dares to approach the gateway to the Underlands?"

Luke sighed. "You've already asked me that!"

"And you still haven't answered."

"Oh, right. It's me, Luke Watson."

The tree thought for a second. "Never heard of you."

"That's because I'm just an ordinary kid," said Luke with a shrug. "Apart from my werewolf thing."

"Werewolf?"

"Yeah," said Luke. "I'm a danger to my friends and family."

"And you've been banished to the Underlands because of that!" roared the tree. "Superduper! Now, if you'll just start begging for your life, we can get on with things."

"No, it's OK," said Luke. "I don't need to beg. I'm kind of banishing myself."

"Really?"

"Yep."

"We've not had that before."

"I can imagine."

"You do know what the Underlands are like?" asked the Gatekeeper.

"Oh, yes," said Luke.

"And that you won't be allowed to come back?"

Luke nodded. "That, too."

The Gatekeeper sighed, his leaves rustling. "Well, I suppose that's everything covered."

"Thanks," said Luke. He peered back into the flaming abyss and took a step forward, just as two large branches swung down to block his way.

"Are you sure you don't want to beg for your life?" the Gatekeeper asked. "Even just a bit?"

"No, I want to go."

The Gatekeeper sniffed, a large drop of sap dribbling down his trunk. "You don't know what it's like," the tree said quietly. "Standing guard over the scorching entrance to an apocalyptic wasteland night and day."

"OK," said Luke. "What is it like?"

"It's lonely!" blubbed the tree, breaking into sobs. "All I want is a little chat to pass the time.

Then you can banish yourself all you like!"

"Fine," said Luke, sitting on the grass. "But let's keep it short. Now, what do you want to chat about?"

The snivelling stopped suddenly, and the split in the Gatekeeper's bark stretched into a wide grin. "Tell me more about how my voice sounds!"

"Ouch!" Dixon glanced down at the bandage covering his finger as he crossed Scream Street's central square, heading home to Sneer Hall. Otto couldn't complain that Dixon hadn't put everything into this particular project. He even had the painful wound to prove it. *Woof! Woof!* Dixon froze at the sound. Dig was coming, followed by Resus and Cleo! Dixon had to find a place to hide.

By the time the pair caught up with Dig, he was sniffing around the base of an ornate iron lamp post. A long, green stripe had been painted down one side.

"Dig!" Cleo exclaimed. "You're supposed to be finding Luke."

Dig narrowed his eyes, growled under his breath and lifted one leg.

"No, no, no!" squealed a voice as the lamp

post began to ripple. Within seconds, Dixon stood, trembling, in its place. "Please don't let the doggy do a wee on me!" he begged.

"Dixon!" snapped Resus. "What are you up to?"

"Yeah," said Cleo. "Why are you acting all nervous?"

Dixon gave an anxious titter. "Nervous? Me? Ha, ha! Claws I'm not nervous — I mean, 'course I'm not nervous! Ahem."

Cleo peered at the bandage wrapped around Dixon's finger. She began to walk around him in a circle. "Broken a nail, have you?"

"What, this?" said Dixon, holding up his hand. "No, it's, er ... it's for ... National Mummy Day!"

Resus blinked. "National what, now?"

"National Mummy Day!" said Dixon, more confidently this time. "It's a way of showing support for the mummies in Scream Street and other G.H.O.U.L. communities. I'm surprised you've not heard of it. All proceeds go to... Yargh!"

The shape-shifter yelled as Cleo grabbed his bandaged hand, twisted it up behind his back, and pinned its whining owner to the floor.

"Looks like you've been impersonating

werewolves," grunted Resus.

"I was only following the mayor's orders!" Dixon wailed.

"You made Luke think he had hurt his family!" spat Cleo. "You snout beetle!"

"Eh?" Both Resus and Dixon turned to look at her.

"Nasty insect. Very common in ancient Egypt," the mummy explained.

"Ohhhh."

Cleo jumped up, leaving the mayor's assistant quaking on the ground. "Now, come on, Dig. Let's go and find Luke!"

Dixon sat up and watched as they disappeared over a garden wall and towards the woods outside Scream Street. What would Otto say now? Worried, he raised his hand to his mouth and made to bite his fingernail.

"Ouch!"

With Dig at point position, it didn't take Cleo and Resus long to pick up Luke's trail. In places where he'd had to travel slowly and cut a path through the undergrowth, they found the going much easier.

"What's Luke doing all the way out here?" asked Resus.

"I think I might know," replied Cleo. "And it's not good. Come on, Dig, let's find Luke now!"

By the time they reached the clearing, Luke was dozing off in front of the chatty Gatekeeper.

"...the Headless Horseman," gossiped the tree, its branches folded in front of it, "now he had a chip on his shoulder about something. And don't talk to me about Ramses the Great! Great, my roots! 'Fine,' I said to him. 'If you want to be buried in a sarcophagus riddled with snout beetles...'"

"There he is!" yelled Cleo, waking her friend with a start.

Luke jumped to his feet. "No!" he yelled. "Don't come any closer!"

"But Luke," called Resus. "It's about your house..."

"I'm never going back there!" Luke shouted, tears pricking at his eyes. "Never!"

Then he turned and jumped straight through the portal into the Underlands.

Chapter Five
THE TRUTH

"Luke!" screamed Cleo, dashing forward. "No!"

"I don't get it!" cried Resus, Dig fretting around his feet and barking. "Where is he? Where's he gone?"

"He has gone whence none shall return!" boomed the Gatekeeper. "Say, are you a mummy? I've got a great story about the time I met—"

"Oh, stick a twig in it!" Cleo snapped.

The tree rustled. "Well, I never."

Cleo began to untie the bandages around her middle. "Quick," she said to Resus. "Hold this and don't let go!"

"OK," said Resus. "But what are you— Oh no! You're not about to do what I think you're about to do, are you?"

"Oh, yes I am!" exclaimed Cleo. Then she raced for the portal and leapt through.

"Right!" commanded the Gatekeeper. "Will everybody please stop banishing themselves to the Underlands? This goes right against the rules, and quite frankly I'm feeling a little delicate after today's proceedings."

The tree turned its eyes down to focus on Resus.

"Don't look at me," said the vampire. "I'm not going anywhere near that thing!"

Then the bandage pulled taut, almost dragging Resus off his feet. The vampire dug his heels into the ground and leaned back, the coarse material burning as it slid through his palms.

"Got ... to ... hold ... it!" He pressed the heel of his shoe against one of the tree's thick roots, flipped his hands to twist the bandage around his wrists and bent back even further.

But the material continued to pull him towards the portal and certain doom.

Dig gripped the end of the bandage in his jaws and added his weight to the effort. Between the vampire and the dog, they managed to slow down Cleo's descent a little, but they were still being dragged towards the flaming hole. "Noooooooooo!" yelled Resus.

"Oh, call me a sentimental old fool," grumbled the Gatekeeper. His branches twisted down and, with long wooden fingers, he lifted Resus and Dig off the ground and yanked hard.

A slightly singed Luke and Cleo came flying out of the portal, landing with a sizzling *thud* on the grass.

The tree dropped Resus and Dig down beside them. Resus was on his feet in a second, throwing his arms around his friends.

He quickly pulled away.

"Ow! You are *hot*!"

Cleo winked at him. "Well, thank you very much."

"Er, n-no," stammered Resus, his cheeks reddening beneath his make up. "I meant that you, er ... you..."

"I know!" said Cleo, rolling her eyes.

"What have you done?" demanded Luke.

"Well," said Cleo, brushing the burned ends from her bandages. "To me, it looks like we risked our lives to save you – again!"

"You don't understand!" cried Luke, tears now rolling down his cheeks. "I'm a monster! A danger to everyone!"

He turned to race back to the portal, but didn't get far. Cleo tackled him to the ground.

"Get off me!"

"No!"

"Let go, Cleo!

"Never!"

"Awkward," commented the Gatekeeper.

Cleo spun Luke over onto his back, and sat on his chest. "Listen to me, you numbskull! It wasn't you who attacked your mum and dad."

"Of course it was!" Luke yelled, struggling to get free. "I was the wolf! I saw the damage! My mum's face!"

He had almost managed to wriggle free when Resus hurried over to join Cleo in sitting on their pal. "You're not the only werewolf in Scream Street, Luke!" he said. "Or, at least, not the only

 56

person who can *look* like one."

Luke stopped squirming and stared up at his friends, just as Dig trotted over and sat on his head.

"What?" he said, through a face full of doggy skeleton.

Cleo and Resus jumped up to help their friend to his feet. Dig paused to give Luke a loving lick, then leapt off too.

"Come with us," said the mummy. "We'll explain on the way."

Tears were running down Otto Sneer's cheeks. Tears of laughter.

"What?" he cried. "Halt the demolitions? Just because you three tell me to? Don't make me laugh! Oh, look, you already have!"

Luke, Resus and Cleo stared up at the mayor, stern-faced. They were back in the banqueting suite of Sneer Hall.

"Well," said Luke. "If you won't listen to us, maybe there's someone else you'll listen to."

"Who?" demanded Otto. "Your werewolf?" NoName appeared at his shoulder. "You don't scare me, boy! And I wouldn't risk transforming

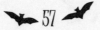

again so soon after what you did to your parents."

"Actually, we had someone else in mind," said Cleo. She pulled a magic wand from the bandages at her side and flicked it in the air.

Behind Otto, the giant magic mirror flickered to life. On the screen, peering down at them, was the imposing face of Greystoke McDread.

"President McDread," said Cleo with a polite smile. "Thank you for joining us at such short notice."

"Well," said McDread. "It sounded important. Now, what's going on?"

"It's Mayor Otto," said Resus. "He's been planning some upgrades to Scream Street."

The President of G.H.O.U.L. twitched his moustache. "And that concerns me because...?"

"The upgrade he's planning is to Sneer Hall," said Luke. "He's going to demolish all the other houses in Scream Street, move the residents into tents, and expand his own property."

"Sneer?" rumbled Greystoke McDread.

But, before the President could say anything else, Otto dropped to his knees before the mirror. "Oh, please forgive me, Greystoke!" he blubbered. "I won't be naughty ever again! I'll give everyone in Scream Street a present — all wrapped up in pretty paper, with a bow on top! *Just forgive me!*"

He sank to the floor, sobbing.

Luke turned to his friends. "Well, that was a little easier than I expected."

"I wouldn't be so sure," said Resus, pointing down at Otto. The trio quickly realized that the mayor wasn't crying. He was laughing again.

"You three must think I'm as thick as a dragon steak!" he said, wiping away his tears. "It was a nice try, though."

"What was?" asked Luke.

Otto continued through his giggles. "I don't know how you persuaded Dixon to impersonate McDread again, but you're not fooling me!"

And with that, Otto began to skip up and down in front of the magic mirror, pulling faces. "Ooh, hello there, President McDread! Or, should I call you President McPoopyHead?"

"What?" demanded the figure in the mirror.

Otto continued. "Sitting there with your big silly nose, and your big silly ears and your ridiculous hair! What an honour it is to see your ugly, rubbery face! Nyah, nyah, nyah!"

"Sneer!"

The mayor paused to blow a raspberry at the screen, then fell about laughing again. "Come on, now. That's enough. Out you come, Dixon!"

"Yes?" said a voice at the opposite end of the room. Otto spun to see his assistant standing in the doorway.

Everything was silent for a few seconds, then Otto made a small squeaking noise. He turned – very slowly – back to the magic mirror, and the furious expression on Greystoke McDread's face.

"Oopsie!"

"Snnneeeeeeeeeerrrrrrrrrr!"

Otto leapt back with a yelp, banking into the table with the model showing the new Scream Street. It flipped over, revealing his scheme in all its glory.

"No! Don't look at that!" he begged, trying desperately to flip the table over again. "It was just a joke! Really! Please forgive me, President McDread, sir! *I can explain.*"

The mayor finally managed to flip the table back over, realizing too late that he'd pushed it far too hard. The table top spun over and over, taking Otto with it.

"Gllaarrk!"

 60

Cleo stepped up to the mirror and smiled. "What Otto is too modest to tell you himself is..."

"...that he's offered everyone in Scream Street something very generous," finished Resus.

Otto's face appeared through the broken model, a tiny ski slope balanced on top of his head. "I have? I mean... Yes, I have!"

"He's also promised to rebuild my parents' house himself – and at his own expense!"

The mayor sobbed.

"Sneer, that's splendid!" declared Greystoke McDread. "Top marks all round – although we must still have a little chat about your, er, *outburst* just then." He sniffed. "President McPoopyHead indeed!"

Otto sank back beneath his table. "Yes, sir."

The President turned back to Luke, Resus and Cleo. "Now, tell me about these generous gifts."

Luke stood with his mum and dad, and watched a very unhappy Otto Sneer climb up a ladder with a stack of roof tiles. Repairs to 13 Scream Street were going well.

"You know," said Mike. "I wasn't really bothered about the upgrades Mayor Sneer

61

promised. I liked our home just the way it was."

"It's nice of him to do all the hard work, isn't it?" said Sue, giving her son a big hug. "Somewhere, deep down, underneath all that unpleasantness, there must beat a warm heart."

"Yeah," said Luke. "Deep, deep, deep down!"

"Luke!" cried a voice.

The Watsons turned to see Resus and Cleo hurrying towards them. With them was NoName, carrying a very large magic mirror and a set of speakers.

"They're here!" said Cleo excitedly.

"Home cinemas, baby!" exclaimed Resus, giving Luke a high-five. "Ours is being installed this afternoon."

Mike ran his fingers over the frame of the new high-definition magic mirror. "Some upgrades are OK, I guess!" he said.

"So," said Luke, grinning at his friends. "What shall we watch first? *Curse of the Mummy's Tomb? Blood-Soaked Vampires 4?*"

"Neither," said Resus.

"We've already picked a movie," said Cleo.

"*Claw of the Werewolf!*" they both cried together.

LIGHT FINGERS

Chapter One
THE CAT

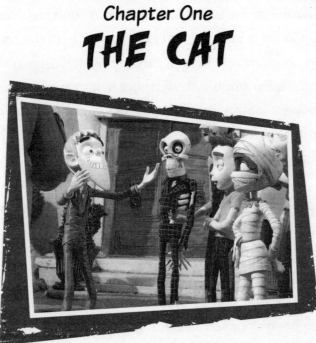

The huge creature stomped along the corridor, priceless works of art on the walls juddering with every clumping footstep. It passed a glistening suit of armour standing to attention in an alcove, its former occupant's battlefield glories long since forgotten. The armour shook as the monster passed, looking for all the world as if it were trembling with fear.

The figure stopped at a small supply closet. Gripping the handle with one large finger and thumb, it swung open the door and reached inside for a large, metal hammer. It held the tool up to examine it, but anyone watching would have been unable to decipher what the creature thought about its find; the beast had no facial features whatsoever. Just an expanse of smooth, blank skin.

Outside, a crowd was gathering. The monster appeared to hear their chatter and turned to look sightlessly out of the window at the increasing mob. Then, gripping the hammer tightly in its fist, it made for the exit.

The mansion's outer doors crashed open, and the beast stepped out among the throng, its fingers twitching around the handle of its weapon. It strode unchallenged through the crowd until it reached a young witch standing against a wooden gatepost. The witch looked up, eyes wide, as the creature raised the hammer high ... then gently tapped a sign in place above her head.

The witch stood back to examine it. "Wow!" said Luella Everwell. "Is that what we're all here to see, NoName?"

NoName, the mayor of Scream Street's bulky bodyguard, slipped the hammer into a loop on his belt and simply pointed at a figure stepping up to a small podium at the front of the audience.

Dixon, Mayor Sir Otto Sneer's assistant, flicked his lank green hair away from his eyes and cleared his throat noisily.

"Roll up, roll up!" he cried. "Come and behold the wonders of ancient Egypt!"

An excited murmur ran through the crowd, as did a small dog. The pooch was all fur and fleas at the front, yet nothing but bones at the back. It sniffed at each pair of feet as it pushed its way through the crowd, pausing to briefly nibble at the glistening white leg of Dr Skully, Scream Street's skeletal schoolteacher and physician.

"Get off, Dig!" Dr Skully cried. "Bad half-dog!"

Growling under his breath, Dig continued to the front of the crowd, where it sat, gnawing at its own back foot.

"And don't miss the star of the show," Dixon continued, gesturing to the sign NoName had just hammered to the gatepost. "The finest relic in G.H.O.U.L.'s collection: the Emerald Cat of Ramennoodle!"

The image on the sign showed a statue of

a cat, a jet-black figure with large, glittering emeralds for eyes. The audience began to *oohh!* and *ahhh!* at the picture – all except Dig, who growled at the potential natural enemy.

"Don't delay!" cried Dixon. "Buy your tickets to see this amazing exhibition now! Drinks and snacks will also be available at a not-so-small price."

As the eager audience lined up to pay the entry fee, NoName reappeared, now wearing a huge cinema usherette's uniform. Slung around his neck was a tray of ice creams and bottles of pop.

Three children were among the last to enter Sneer Hall. Dig wagged his tail excitedly and made to follow them, but NoName stepped in the partial pooch's way and held up another sign. This one showed the silhouette of a dog, crossed out with a diagonal red line.

Dig spun to wiggle his bony back end indignantly. But NoName just shrugged and spun the sign around. On the other side was a half-skeletal dog with a line through it.

Dig turned and slunk away.

Inside Sneer Hall, Mayor Sir Otto Sneer stood at one end of his vast banqueting hall, rubbing his hands together. The rest of the huge room was filled with glass cases and marble plinths, each displaying a different ancient Egyptian relic. The crowd milled among them, soaking up the beauty of another age.

Behind the mayor, on a giant magic mirror, appeared the face of Greystoke McDread, the President of Government Housing of Unusual Lifeforms, or G.H.O.U.L.

"I must say, Sneer," said McDread, "it is awfully nice of you to exhibit the Emerald Cat in your own home."

Otto reached out to stroke the cat, which sat on a nearby plinth. "My pleasure, President McDread," he crooned. "Such a valuable artefact should be displayed for all to see."

"Quite so!" agreed McDread. "Well, take good care of it, won't you?" With a hiss, the image on the magic mirror disappeared.

"Oh, I'll look after it all right!" muttered Otto to himself.

The stream of visitors reached the jewel in the exhibition's crown. Within minutes, the Emerald

Cat was surrounded by cooing admirers.

"It's so shiny!" sighed Luella, staring at her reflection in the statue's glimmering emeralds.

"I've never seen anything quite so beautiful!" sobbed Dr Skully.

"What an utter pile of—" Luke Watson clamped a hand over the mouth of his mummy friend, Cleo Farr. With the help of Resus Negative, a young vampire, he dragged Cleo to the back of the room, where Luke removed his hand.

"What did you do that for?" Cleo demanded with a scowl.

"To stop you getting yourself into trouble!" replied Luke. "You can't just go around spouting your mouth off like that."

Cleo paced up and down, angrily. "Unbelievable," she grumbled. "What right does Otto Sneer have to parade valuables stolen from my great-great-great-great-great-great-grandfather's tomb?"

Resus counted the number of "greats" on his fingers. "What, you mean Pharaoh Ramennoodle was your great-great-great-great... Hang on, I've lost count."

Cleo nodded. "All this belonged to him."

"Well, it's cool stuff," said Resus, leading his friends through the assorted exhibits. "Look – canopic jars, a model slave ship, a sarcophagus lid!" He picked up an item about the size of a hairbrush, with nasty-looking, partially rusted blades extruding from one end. "I bet this was used for mummifying bodies!"

"Er, Resus..." began Cleo.

But Resus was lost in his imagination. He raised the relic to his nose and sniffed hard. "Yes! I can totally still smell the brain juice on it!"

Otto Sneer appeared and snatched the item from his hand. "Dixon!" he roared. "How many times have I told you not to leave my nose-hair clippers lying around?"

A smile broke out on Cleo's face for the first time that morning. Despite being born to vampire parents, Resus was a normal boy. To blend in with his family, he clipped on fake fangs, dyed his hair black and wore pale make up. Bent double and gagging, Resus didn't need the make up now.

"Come on," said Luke. "I want to take a closer look at this cat everyone's getting so excited about."

He and Cleo led the way to the plinth where the Emerald Cat was sitting. Resus followed, cleaning his nostrils with the corner of his vampire cape.

"Look at it," breathed Cleo, as they surrounded the priceless statue. "It's so beautiful." She reached out a bandaged hand to touch it, only to have it slapped away by Dixon.

"No touching the exhibits!" he snapped, instantly regretting his tone when he saw the thunderous expression on Cleo's face.

"This cat," she said through gritted teeth, "is family property!"

"Well, I can't see your name on it anywhere," said Dixon, as bravely as he could.

Cleo smiled sweetly at Dixon.

"Oh, dear," said Luke. "Dixon's in for it now."

"Yep," Resus agreed. "I almost prefer a scowling Cleo to when she smiles like that."

"Dixon," said Cleo. "Nowhere in this Egyptian exhibition does it explain how someone is mummified."

Dixon swallowed hard. "I–Isn't there?"

"Do you know how people are mummified?"

"Er... Nope!"

"Oh, it's such fun!" beamed Cleo. "First of all, the body is cut open and all internal organs removed. Then that empty space is filled with stuffing and sawdust."

Dixon blinked, not looking too well.

"Then, they push long spikes up the nose and pull the brain out through the nostrils." The mummy's smile vanished. "Which is exactly what I'm going to do to you if Otto Sneer doesn't stop making money off the back of my family's belongings!"

Dixon clamped a hand over his mouth and ran for the exit. And, for the second time in half an hour, Luke and Resus were forced to pull their friend away from the star of the show.

"We'd better get out of here!" Luke said. With another scowl, Cleo began to stomp towards the exit.

"If you're leaving, don't forget to purchase not-at-all-tacky souvenirs!" announced Sir Otto. He gestured to NoName, whose tray was now filled with mugs, caps and T-shirts, all featuring an image of the Emerald Cat. "What better way to remember your visit than with—"

"The Emerald Cat!" yelled Dixon, as he reappeared from the restroom, pointing. "It's been stolen!"

Everyone in the crowd turned to stare at the now-empty plinth.

"Bar the doors!" roared Otto. "No one leaves!"

Chapter Two
THE ESCAPE

Cleo strode towards the doors of the banqueting suite, only to find her path blocked by NoName. "Let me out, you big lump of nothing!" she snapped.

Otto was behind her in a second. "Why so eager to leave, young Cleo?" he asked. "Something to hide, perhaps?"

"No!" Cleo replied. "I just don't want to watch you showing off *my* family's stuff."

"Sounds like a motive to me!" sneered Sneer.

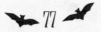

"Dixon, play the security tape."

Dixon pulled a magic wand from his inside pocket and waved it in front of the giant magic mirror. A black-and-white recording of the Emerald Cat came into view. Everyone in the room watched the video intently, occasionally casting suspicious glances in Cleo's direction.

The video showed Dixon racing for the restroom, hand over his mouth. Visitors continued to walk in and out of the video frame, admiring the precious statue.

"See!" cried Cleo. "I didn't take anything!"

Just then, a hand wrapped in bandages appeared on the screen. It reached in from among the busy crowd and snatched the cat from its plinth.

"There!" bellowed Sir Otto as Dixon paused the image.

"That wasn't me!" exclaimed Cleo.

"Well, I don't see any other mummies in the room," snarled Otto. "And you *were* the one who made Dixon abandon his guard duty. Come on, hand it over!"

"But, I—" Before Cleo could finish, NoName grabbed her and spun her upside down. He held her by the ankles and shook hard.

"See!" said Luke, when nothing fell out. "It wasn't her!"

"Bah," grumbled the mayor as NoName set Cleo down again. "That just means she's already smuggled it out of here. At least we have the thief, and she can be punished."

"Punished?" said Resus, stepping forward. "But she didn't do it!"

"You've no evidence," added Luke. "Leave her alone!"

"I'd stay back if I were you!" Otto warned the boys. "Unless you want to be banished to the Underlands as well!"

Cleo turned to face her friends and stared. "The Underlands?" she croaked.

Deep in the woods outside Scream Street, Luke was on his knees using his huge werewolf paws to dig a large hole.

Since moving to the unusual community, he had gradually been able to fine-tune his ability to transform just one part of his body at a time. Ten minutes ago, his hands had been boringly human. Now, a pair of vast, fur-covered paws tipped with long talons was excavating huge mounds of earth.

Resus sat on a fallen tree trunk and watched. "Are we sure..." he began.

"Sure about what?" asked Luke, not pausing to look up from his work.

"Are we sure that Cleo *didn't* take the Emerald Cat?" the vampire asked. "I mean, she did seem pretty cross, and, well ... the camera never lies."

This time, Luke did stop and look up. "If she says she didn't do it, then she didn't do it."

Resus sighed. "I know," he said. "But we're going to have a hard job proving her innocence, especially now she's been sentenced to banishment in the Underlands."

Luke concentrated on transforming his hands back to normal, and hoped that Resus hadn't noticed him shudder. The Underlands were a terrible, desolate place, far below Scream Street, where all the criminal monsters who couldn't be controlled were sent. The endless miles of dead landscape were home to odious ogres, terrible trolls, and many more wicked and dangerous creatures.

The trio knew that once you were sent through the portal there was almost no way back from the Underlands. Rumours claimed that the villains banished there had made makeshift towns to survive — dreadful, lawless places where the strong picked on the weak, and where the slightest disagreement might result in a battle to the death.

"That's why we're doing this," said Luke, dragging a leafy branch to rest over the large hole. "Now, help me get this thing covered up."

Resus and Luke had just finished making sure their trap looked no different to the undergrowth around it when they heard the sound of an approaching cart.

"Quick!" hissed Luke, pulling Resus behind a nearby bush.

The pair watched as a cart approached, pulled by NoName. Dixon sat at the back, holding the reins. Behind him was a cage, inside which Cleo was trapped.

"You'd better let me out of here, Dixon, or you'll be sorry," she growled, clutching at the metal bars.

"Not a chance, criminal!" said Dixon, safe in the knowledge that Cleo couldn't reach him where he was sitting. At least, that's what he hoped.

 81

"OK," hissed Luke to Resus. "I'll keep them busy, and you bust Cleo out of the cage."

"No problem," said Resus. Then he thought for a second. "Hang on, how am I supposed to..."

But Luke had already disappeared among the trees.

Resus took a deep breath. "OK," he said to himself. "I guess we're playing this one by ear!"

Back on the cart, Cleo was still ranting from within the cage.

"Do you really think you'll get away with this, Dixon?" she yelled.

"It's not my fault," Dixon retorted. "I'm only doing what Otto told— Ow!"

He pulled the reins to stop NoName as a large pinecone bounced off his head. Dixon picked it up and looked around.

"Hey, who threw— Oww!"

Another pinecone, bigger than the first, hit him on the ear.

"Whoever is doing that, you'd better stop it right— Oooowww!"

That pinecone was particularly spiky, and it bounced off Dixon's nose.

Luke leapt out of the bushes ahead of them

and blew a raspberry. "Hey," he cried, aiming two pinecones directly at NoName. "You two uglies are great for target practice!"

Dixon ducked to avoid another hail of pinecones and shouted: "There's room in this cage for you too, you know!"

"You'll have to catch me first!" teased Luke, hurling another pair of pinecones at Cleo's captors.

"Right!" snapped Dixon, jumping down from the cart. "NoName – after him!"

NoName turned and gestured towards Cleo, who was watching and laughing from her cage.

"She's safe for now!" Dixon bellowed. "Just get after Luke!"

As Luke turned and headed into the undergrowth, Resus raced out of the bushes and leapt onto the cart.

"Resus!" Cleo cried.

"I'm here to get you out," said the vampire.

"Thank you!" said Cleo. "Er, how?"

Resus smiled weakly. "I was hoping you might have some ideas on that."

"Oh, boy," sighed Cleo, rubbing her face with a bandaged palm.

 83

Deep in the undergrowth, Luke trotted onwards, turning occasionally to throw more pinecones – and insults – back in the direction of Dixon and NoName. "I normally wouldn't mind being captured by a pair of clowns like you two, but it's the smell I'd hate. You stink like a pair of goblin's underpants!"

"How did you know I get my underpants from goblins?" Dixon demanded. He and NoName were almost on Luke. One last push and they would have him in their clutches.

Suddenly, Luke leapt up and, with a pair of rapidly transformed werewolf arms, grabbed hold of a branch that overhung the narrow trail. "Yahoo!" he cried.

Both Dixon and NoName watched him swing over a seemingly harmless patch of ground, and chased after him. That's when they fell through the fake floor of branches and leaves into the deep pit Luke had dug.

"Oh, dear!" Dixon groaned as he uncurled himself from the jumble of arms and legs at the bottom of the hole. "The mayor isn't going to like this one little bit."

Back at the cart, Resus was pulling a seemingly

endless stream of useless objects out of his magic vampire cloak. He tossed the items into the bushes as they appeared.

"Piece of celery... Matchstick boat... One boxing glove... Doorstop... Bolt-cutters... Teddy bear... Fondue set..." He lifted the side of the cloak and glared inside. "You'd better give me something useful soon, or I *will* turn you into curtains!"

"Resus," interrupted Cleo, her patience unravelling fast.

"What?"

Cleo pointed to where he had thrown the bolt-cutters.

"Oh!" said the vampire. He leapt out of the cart and into the bushes after them.

Luke dashed up to the cart. He slid one of his still wolf-like claws into the cage and picked the lock.

"Come on!" he said, as Cleo leapt down to the ground beside him. "We have to find out what's happening here."

Cleo raced after him in the direction of Scream Street's central square.

"Got them!" yelled Resus happily, as he

battled his way out of the bushes and pulled loose twigs from his hair. He raced around the cart, bolt-cutters at the ready, only to find the cage empty and the woods silent.

"Oh, come on!" he groaned, looking around. "*Now* where is she?"

"Resus!" came the mummy's voice from the distance. "This way!"

Tucking the bolt-cutters back inside his cloak, Resus ran in the direction of the voice.

"Coming!"

As Resus dodged the pit, Dixon called out to him. "Resus, my old mate! Can you help us out of here?" There was a long silence as the vampire vanished down the trail. "Nope, he's gone. OK, NoName, it's down to you. Just remember not to throw me too hard, or— Aaarrrgggh!"

Dixon was hurled from the pit. He flew into the air, crashing through the tree branches and coming to land inside the cage on the back of his own cart. "Oof!"

The door closed and locked with a heavy *click!*

"Mayor Otto's *really* not going to like this," he groaned.

Chapter Three
THE GUEST

Luke picked the lock to Sneer Hall and led Resus and Cleo back to the exhibition in the banqueting suite.

"What are we doing back here?" hissed Cleo.

"We need to find out who really stole the Emerald Cat," whispered Luke, "or we'll all end up in the Underlands once Dixon tells Otto what we did."

"Well," said Resus, "technically, I didn't know what you were planning, and I didn't help

Cleo escape from the cage, so I shouldn't be—"
He stopped to find both his friends glaring at him.
"Oh, all right," he sighed. "I'm in."

The trio dropped to their hands and knees
and began to search around the glass cases and
plinths.

"What are we looking for?" asked Resus.

"Clues," replied Cleo. "Anything that might
explain who really took the Emerald Cat."

Resus spotted movement in the shadows up
ahead. Something thin and white was flicking in
and out of a shaft of light. Silently, the vampire
crept closer, then pounced. He was rewarded by
a big, slobbery lick on his cheek.

"I've found Dig!" he said, letting go of the
pooch's skeletal tail.

"What are you doing in here, boy?" asked
Luke, tickling Dig behind the ear. "Looking for
the Emerald Cat, like us?"

Cleo reached the magic mirror and stood.
She snatched up the magic wand and turned the
screen on, rewinding the security footage to the
point when the artefact had been snatched. She,
Resus and Luke watched the video three times.

"Sorry," Resus said to Cleo. "It really does

look like a mummy's arm taking it."

Dig began to growl softly.

"Sssh!" said Luke. "Someone's coming!"

Cleo flicked the wand to deactivate the magic mirror, then the trio darted behind it to hide.

Dixon and NoName came in through the doors at the far end of the room. The mayor's huge henchman was covered in dirt, as though he'd had to dig himself out of a particularly deep hole in the ground.

"OK," said Dixon to the bodyguard, "here's the plan. We'll tell Mayor Otto it was all your fault. Any objections, speak now!"

NoName could only shrug.

"Thanks, buddy," said Dixon, patting the monster on his arm. "I knew you'd take the rap for me."

Behind the magic mirror, Dig began to sniff at the air. "What is it, boy?" Luke asked, trying to keep a grip on the half-hound. But Dig wriggled free and trotted back out among the exhibits.

"Come back!" hissed Cleo, but it was too late.

"I can reach him!" whispered Resus, lunging forward, hand outstretched to grab hold of Dig's tail. But he missed and bumped into one of the

tall pedestals. On top of the plinth, an ancient canopic jar began to wobble.

Luke and Cleo managed to drag Resus back to their hiding place just before the jar crashed to the floor.

"Hello?" cried Dixon. "Who's there?"

As Luke, Resus and Cleo watched, a mummy's arm reached out from behind a golden casket and pushed Dig out to where Dixon and NoName were standing.

"Oi!" Dixon yelled. "No dogs in here! You've been told!"

He and NoName chased Dig out of the banqueting suite and off towards the main doors of Sneer Hall.

After a moment's silence, the three friends stood and wearily made their way towards the golden casket.

"Thanks for helping us," said Luke. "The bad guys have gone now. You can come out if you like."

Slowly, the bandaged arm snaked into view.

"Does the rest of you want to come out, too?" asked Resus.

The arm paused for a second, then appeared

completely from behind the casket.

"Oh," said Resus. "There *is* no rest of you. You're just an arm!"

Cleo crouched and reached out to shake the hand at the end of the severed limb. "I'm Cleo Farr," she said. "Who are you?"

Niles Farr, Cleo's dad, stood in his ornately decorated living room and peered sadly at an image inside a golden frame. "Once I was one of the greatest men in Egypt!" he sighed. "Now, all I have to remember that time by is this final portrait."

Cleo opened the door behind him. "I've told you before, Dad, that's a mirror!" Luke and Resus entered behind her.

"Darling, you're back!" cried Niles, spinning around to give his daughter a hug. "And you've brought your friends with you!"

"Not just my friends, Dad," said Cleo. "Someone new as well. Or, I think they might actually be someone very, very old."

She handed over the severed mummified arm.

"Could it be?" Niles gasped. "Great-Great-Great-Great-Great-Grandfather Ramennoodle?

I don't believe it!"

Resus tried counting on his fingers again. "I'm not sure that's the right number of greats," he muttered.

"We found him at Sneer Hall," Cleo explained.

Niles scowled at the hand. "What were you doing there?" he asked.

The arm leapt out of Niles's clutch and hopped up beside a burning oil lamp. It began to wiggle its fingers, making different shapes with the shadows cast on the far wall.

"Ooh, I'm good at this game!" Resus cried. "I'll translate." The vampire watched intently as the hand twisted and turned to make image after image.

"Got it!" said Resus at last. "Ramennoodle was carried here by a bird, hidden inside a coconut that was swallowed by a crocodile, then rescued by a rabbit that made toasted cheese sandwiches."

"You might like that game," said Luke kindly, "but you stink at it."

"Here," said Cleo, grabbing a reed brush and a pot of ink and presenting them to the arm.

 92

"Perhaps you could write it down instead?"

The hand gripped the brush, spun it in its fingers, dipped the tip in the ink and began to scrawl lines of hieroglyphics on the wall.

Resus squinted at the bizarre pictures. "Well, that's a lot clearer."

"Hush!" said Cleo. "I can read it... Emerald Cat ... stolen from tomb long ago ... arms stolen, too!"

"Eww!" said Resus.

"All sold to G.H.O.U.L...." Cleo continued. "Kept safe until Otto offered to display them at Sneer Hall."

The hand stopped writing and gave Cleo a thumbs-up.

"So, where's the *other* arm?" Luke asked.

The severed arm went back to work, Cleo still translating. "Otto has kept the other arm at Sneer Hall," she said. "He threatened to hurt it — unless this arm helped him to steal the Emerald Cat!"

"So, Otto's got the cat!" said Luke.

"I don't mean to sound uncaring," said Resus. "But how, exactly, can Otto hurt a dismembered arm?"

The hand quivered, then drew an image

everyone could understand – a severed arm being held over a roaring fire.

"He... He was going to burn your other arm?" Cleo cried.

The hand gave her a thumbs-up.

"That monster!" spat Cleo, heading for the door. "I'll teach him."

Niles grabbed his daughter and held her back. "No," he said. "Our family does not exact revenge upon its enemies."

Cleo frowned. "But you did all the time back in Egypt, when you were in power."

"And I have learned my lesson, my child," said Niles. "Now, how about we all sit down and relax with a nice pot of plume thistle tea?"

"Er, I'd rather drink that pot of ink, thanks," said Resus.

"I don't think there's going to be a lot of ink left," said Luke. "The artist is back at it."

Taking a deep breath, Cleo made her way back to the wall and continued to translate what the hand of Ramennoodle was painting. "He says this arm was forced to creep among the crowd when the exhibition opened and to snatch the Emerald Cat at the first sign of a distraction."

"What distraction?" asked Resus. "I don't remember a... Oh, hang on..."

"What?" asked Cleo.

Luke rested a hand on his friend's bandaged shoulder. "You had an argument with Dixon," he said. "You threatened to mummify him, and he ran off looking unwell."

Cleo sank into an armchair. "It *was* me," she said quietly. "*I* caused the distraction that allowed Otto to steal the Emerald Cat."

"It wasn't your fault," said Luke gently. "You were angry at Otto for displaying your family's belongings."

Cleo wiped her eyes with the back of her hand. "Now we'll never see the Emerald Cat again."

"What do you think, Mr Farr?" Luke asked.

Niles stared at the wall of hieroglyphics. "I think there's no way that ink will ever wash off," he said.

"Hang on," said Resus. "Where's the other arm now?"

Ramennoodle's hand grabbed the brush again and drew one final picture — a row of tombstones.

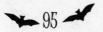

"The graveyard!" said Cleo, jumping to her feet. "We might not be able to get the Emerald Cat back, but we can rescue the other half of what's left of Great-Great-Great-Great-Great-Great-Granddad!"

Once again, Niles blocked her path. "No," he said flatly. "This adventure is over, Cleo. I do not want you returned to me in pieces, like your great-great-great-great-great-great-grandfather."

"I got five – no, six, 'greats' that time," said Resus.

"OK, Dad, you're right." said Cleo. "Hey, why don't you go and make up the spare room for Ramennoodle? You could use those new lily-scented candles you bought at Eefa's Emporium last week."

"A marvellous idea!" exclaimed Niles, heading up the stairs.

Cleo chuckled. "Works every time."

By the time Niles had remembered that their house didn't have a spare bedroom and had returned to the living room, Cleo, her friends and the amputated arm of his ancient ancestor were all gone.

"Oh," he said.

Chapter Four

THE CRYPT

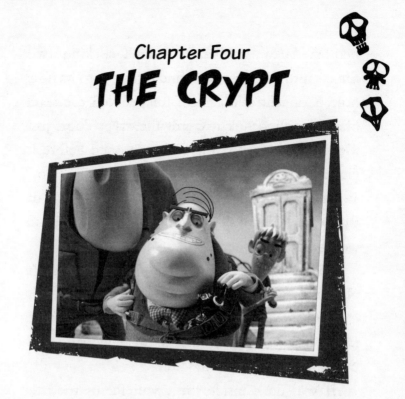

Luke, Resus, Cleo and the arm of Ramennoodle hid behind a large tombstone in the graveyard and watched as NoName approached the ornate doorway to the Sneer family crypt. The bulky bodyguard knocked on the door with his vast knuckles. After a brief wait, the entrance to the crypt swung open.

NoName slipped inside, and the door began to close. Ramennoodle tapped Luke on the shoulder and gestured towards a skull lying

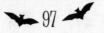

nearby. Luke grabbed the skull, sticking two fingers into its eye sockets and a third into its nose hole. Concentrating hard, Luke rolled the skull like a bowling ball towards the crypt door, just managing to wedge the entrance open before it closed completely.

"Come on," he whispered, leading the way to the crypt. "Thanks!" he said to the skinless head as he stepped inside.

"No worries," said the skull. "I wasn't planning on doing much today, anyway. Just a bit of sitting around and thinking about stuff. Don't be too long, though: I don't want to end up with a skull-ache!"

It was dark inside the crypt. Resus tried to produce a flaming torch from inside his cloak, but he only managed to extract a screwdriver, a piece of stinky cheese and a cupcake. The group held hands to avoid being separated, and continued deeper into the tomb.

They emerged inside the main room of the crypt, which was lit by flickering candles and filled with empty plinths and pictureless picture frames.

"Looks to me like someone's planning their

own private art gallery," said Luke.

"Yeah," agreed Cleo, pointing, "a *stolen* art gallery. Look!"

There, standing on the centremost plinth, was the Emerald Cat.

Cleo dashed forward to grab it.

"No, wait!" cried Resus. He reached out to stop her, but it was too late. Cleo snatched the priceless artefact from its stand and held it tightly in her arms.

"This is never going anywhere, ever again!" she said firmly.

The surface of the Emerald Cat began to ripple, and the relic started to grow in size and change form. A few seconds later, Cleo found herself hugging Scream Street's resident shape-shifter, Dixon.

"Yuck!" she squealed, jumping back and wiping her hands on her bandages.

"Yuck?" repeated Dixon. "Thanks a lot!"

"I thought you were the Emerald Cat!" snapped Cleo.

"No," said Dixon, grinning. "I'm just the guy who caught you!"

A large shadow fell over the room as NoName

99

appeared from one of the alcoves, closely followed by Mayor Sir Otto Sneer. He was clutching the real Emerald Cat in his hands.

"You freaks are so predictable!" he scoffed. "I knew you'd come here, looking for this. Did you think I was stupid?"

"Well..." began Resus.

"It was a rhetorical question!" barked Otto.

"You stole the cat and made everyone think that Cleo had taken it!" said Luke angrily. "You almost had her banished to the Underlands!"

"Almost," sighed Otto. "But not quite. Still, there's always next time." He opened his jacket and slipped the statue of the Emerald Cat inside his pocket, creating a very large, visible lump.

Cleo darted forward, but NoName stepped in her way and pulled Ramennoodle's second arm from a sack at his side.

"Look!" hissed Resus. "It's your great-great-great- ... great... Oh, whatever! It's your granddad's other arm!"

"Give it here, NoName," growled Cleo. But, after a nod from Otto, the heavyweight henchman dangled the old limb over one of the candle flames. The ancient bandages began to sizzle.

"Well, well, well," cackled Otto. "It appears that, as usual, I have the upper hand! Ahahahahaha!" He looked from Dixon to NoName and back — but neither of his sidekicks got the joke. "Typical," he sighed, and pushed Dixon in the direction of the exit.

NoName, meanwhile, moved Ramennoodle's arm away from the flame and ushered the three friends back into a corner of the room.

"Far be it for me to keep a family apart," Otto said. He snatched the second arm from his minder and tossed it towards the trio.

Resus caught it, and the two mummified arms twisted around each other in a happy hug.

"What about us?" demanded Luke.

Otto grinned. "Oh, I thought you three might like to spend a bit of time with *my* family for a change," he said, gesturing to a number of stone coffins at the far end of the room. "I'll come back and let you out in, say ... fifty or sixty years?"

Reaching the exit, Otto kicked the skull out of way.

"Ow!" it cried. "There's no need for that!"

Once NoName and Dixon had joined him outside, the mayor let the door to the crypt swing shut.

Luke raced for the exit, diving to try to stop it from completely closing, but he was too late.

Thud!

The gust of wind from the closing door blew out all the candles, plunging the tomb into darkness. The kids − and Ramennoodle's arms − were trapped inside.

"No!" roared Luke, pounding on the door. "Otto! Let us out!"

"OK," said Cleo. "Don't panic." She took a deep breath. "Luke, calm down. Resus, try your cloak again. See if it will be a bit more helpful in finding us some light this time."

"I'll give it a go," said Resus. "But it's hard enough when I can actually see what I'm pulling out of the pesky thing!"

"I can't believe Otto has shut us in here!" bellowed Luke.

"I said calm down, Luke!" Cleo urged. "Resus, how's it going?"

"Not brilliantly," the vampire replied in the dark. "I think that's a pot of yoghurt. That's definitely a wooden spoon. Hang on... This thing has got a switch, whatever it is!"

"Turn it on!" cried Cleo.

Suddenly, the entire crypt was flooded with flashing red, blue and yellow disco lights. A pop music beat echoed off the walls, the lights pulsing in time.

"Ahem!" said Resus. "Not exactly the mood I was going for, but it's better than nothing."

But Cleo wasn't looking at him. She was pointing into the shadows and trembling. "Oh n-no," she stammered. "Resus..."

The vampire swallowed hard. "Do I really want to know what you're about to tell me?"

An inhuman snarl rang out, and a large shadow began to emerge from the far end of the crypt. An outline of thick fur turned red, yellow and blue beneath the disco lights.

"Oh, Luke, you haven't," sighed Resus.

Luke's fully formed werewolf jumped out of the darkness and howled.

Hoowwwwwlllll! "Maybe he just really likes disco music and fancies a dance," suggested Cleo weakly.

With a mighty roar, the werewolf lunged straight for Resus and Cleo. There was nowhere to go. The pair ran laps around the crypt, chased

every step of the way by their furious furry friend.

Left unnoticed by the werewolf, the twin arms of Ramennoodle started digging up through the bare earth ceiling of the crypt with their hands. At one point, the left arm paused to click its fingers in time with the pounding pop tune, until the right slapped its wrist. The offending digits got back to work.

"This is getting ridiculous!" yelled Cleo, as she and Resus began their fourth circuit of the tomb.

"And I'm getting dizzy!" shouted Resus.

"RROOOAAARR!" bellowed the werewolf.

Waiting for just the right moment, Cleo leapt into the air and flipped over backwards. She landed behind the werewolf as Resus hurled random items from the inside of his vampire cloak over his shoulder: a bathroom sponge, a comic book and a tub of wart cream.

"Oh, where's a great big wolf trap when you need one?" he cried. "I could do with a hand here."

Ramennoodle's right hand stopped digging and pounced, landing on the back of the werewolf's neck. It quickly pressed its palm firmly over the creature's eyes.

Luke's wolf stopped chasing Resus and twisted from side to side, trying to swat the hand from its face. But the arm was too quick. It scuttled up to tap on one shoulder, then slid down the werewolf's furry leg to tickle its feet.

Resus was finally able to stop running and catch his breath. He spotted Cleo, clawing at the hole in the ceiling alongside Ramennoodle's left hand. "What are you doing?" he demanded.

"Trying to dig our way out of here!" Cleo snapped. "Wait, that's it! Dig! I need a bone." She raced to the far end of the crypt, and began to slide open the lid of one of the stone coffins. Resus joined her to help push.

"You really think this is the right time for a spot of grave robbing?" he asked.

But Cleo didn't reply. Instead, she pushed her arm into the coffin and... *Snap!* When she pulled it back out, she was clutching a leg bone.

"Sorry, whoever you are!" she said. She turned to the left arm: "You go and help your twin distract the wolf!"

While the dismembered arms of her great-great-great-great-great-great-grandfather poked and prodded Luke's werewolf, Cleo pushed the bone as far up the tunnel as she could.

"I really wish someone would explain what's going on," said Resus.

"Ssshh!" said Cleo. "Listen."

From the other end of the tunnel, there came a scraping, then a sniffing, and then a familiar furry face appeared, its tongue snaking out to lick at the juicy leg bone in Cleo's hand.

"Dig!" cried Resus. "It's you! Up in the graveyard!"

"Yep!" said Cleo. "You can always rely on Dig to sniff out a tasty treat."

As the half-skeletal dog and Cleo worked to widen the hole to the surface, a voice echoed out behind them. "When did we open some kind of underground nightclub?"

Resus and Cleo turned to find Luke sitting on the floor, back in human form and with the arms of Ramennoodle sitting alongside him.

"We'll explain once we're out of here," said Cleo. "Not much further to go. Then all we have to do to prove our innocence is get the Emerald Cat back from Otto. Easy!"

"That actually sounds really hard," said Resus. "What's the plan?"

"I think I know," said Luke, joining his friends at the makeshift tunnel.

"Well, I don't," said Resus. "How are we going to do it?"

Luke grinned. "We're going to confess!"

Chapter Five

THE CONFESSION

NoName lumbered out of Sneer Hall's main doors and reached up to take down the exhibition sign featuring the picture of the Emerald Cat.

Just then, a blur of fur and bone whizzed past him, yapping madly. NoName spun and tried to swat Dig with the sign as he raced past, but missed. By the time the bodyguard turned around again, the semi-dog was back, gnawing at his ankle.

NoName clenched his fists — the only sign

that he was anything but calm and complacent — and chased Dig across the gardens of Sneer Hall.

Once he had gone, Luke, Resus and Cleo were able to sneak inside the building with the twin arms of Ramennoodle. They paused at the doorway of the banqueting suite and peeked inside to find Mayor Sneer pacing up and down in front of the giant magic mirror. On the screen was the very stern face of G.H.O.U.L.'s president, Greystoke McDread.

"Oh, President McDread!" cried Otto dramatically, the back of his hand pressed against his forehead. "The Emerald Cat — stolen!"

"Yes," rumbled McDread. "So you've been saying for the past fifteen minutes."

"I apologize, your Presidentness!" exclaimed Otto. "It's just that ... somewhere deep down, I can't help but feel this is *my* fault! Crazy, I know."

McDread rolled his eyes. "We know it's not your fault," he said. "You've made that perfectly clear. These thieves you've described sound very cunning."

"Oh, but they were!" said Otto, eyes wide at

the memory of the event. "It's just such a shame that they will never, ever be found!"

"I wouldn't be so sure about that!" said Cleo as she, Resus and Luke popped up behind the mayor.

Otto squealed and jumped.

"What?" bellowed McDread. "What's going on here?"

"We're the thieves," said Luke, matter-of-factly.

"You're the thieves?" blustered the President.

"Yep!" said Resus. "We're the thieves!"

"Hang on," said Otto, scowling. "*You're* the thieves?"

"Is there an echo in here?" Cleo asked.

"Stop!" ordered McDread. "Everybody stop talking. And especially stop claiming to be the thieves."

"But, we *are* the thieves," Cleo insisted. "We took the Emerald Cat!"

"That's right," said Resus. "We simply can't live with the guilt, so we've come to return it."

"Well, that's that sorted!" declared McDread. "I expect you can handle it yourself at this point, Sneer."

"No, wait!" said Otto, looking confused.

"These three frea— Er, I mean frea-endly young people *can't* have come here to return the Emerald Cat."

"And why not?" asked Cleo, with a smile.

Otto ran his fingers over the bulge in his jacket. "Because I... Oh! Er... I don't believe they are telling the truth, Mr President."

The face of Greystoke McDread glared down at Otto. "Are you quite well, Sneer?" he demanded. "You have turned a ghastly shade of green."

"He's just thinking about the emerald gems covering the cat, Mr President," said Cleo. "You see—"

Suddenly, the two severed arms leapt from beneath Resus's cloak and grabbed onto Otto's trouser legs. As the mayor squirmed, they picked their way up to his shoulders, where one arm opened his jacket, and the other plucked the Emerald Cat from his inside pocket.

"Oh, my word!" said Otto with a gulp. "How on earth did that get in there?"

"Sneer!" thundered Greystoke McDread. "You had better have a *very* good explanation for this."

 111

"Well, you see, sir," began Otto. Then he sighed, and his shoulders slumped. "No. I've got nothing."

"But I have," said Luke, stepping forward.

Otto scowled. "You do?"

Luke nodded. "You see, Mr President, Otto hired us to steal the Emerald Cat from the exhibition."

"I did?" said Otto quizzically. "I mean, yes, I did!"

"He wanted to prove that these ancient artefacts aren't safe in G.H.O.U.L.'s possession," Luke continued.

"Is this true, Sneer?" McDread demanded.

"Er... Yes, sir. I think?"

"In fact," said Resus. "Otto was telling us that, really, the Emerald Cat and all the other ancient relics should be returned to their rightful owner, the late Pharaoh Ramennoodle."

"This is him here, sir," said Cleo. "Well, about ten per cent of him, anyway."

Both arms waved cheerily in the direction of the magic mirror. Greystoke McDread forced a thin smile and waved back.

"Yes," he said, after a moment's thought. "I

can see this was a very well thought-out plan. Well done, Sneer."

"Thank you, Mr President," said Otto, confused.

"And I agree that the Emerald Cat should be returned to its rightful owner."

"No!" cried Otto, grabbing the Cat back and clinging tightly to it. "I mean... *No* question about it, sir!"

The bandaged hands clapped for a few seconds, then drummed their fingers on Otto's shoulders while they waited. The trio grinned as the mayor very reluctantly released his grip on the statue. In the end, Ramennoodle's left hand had to prise Otto's fingers away from the artefact.

"And don't forget the rest of this gentleman's belongings," said McDread on the screen. "I hope I can trust you to have everything securely packed up and returned to Ramennoodle's pyramid in Egypt."

"But, the cost..." began Otto.

"You can use the money you made selling tickets for the exhibition," said McDread. "That should just about cover it."

Otto sniffed, and a tear rolled down one cheek. "Yes, sir," he croaked.

"Plus, I presume you agreed to pay our young friends here for their part in such an elaborate deception," said McDread.

For a brief moment, Cleo, Luke and Resus thought Otto might faint.

"No, that's OK, Mr President," said Cleo. "We're just happy to see the artefacts returned to where they really belong."

Greystoke McDread nodded. "Just talk to me next time, Sneer," he said. "There really is no need for all this drama!"

With a hiss, the image on the magic mirror disappeared.

Utterly deflated, Otto sank to the floor. "Whatever you say, sir," he muttered.

The two dismembered arms handed the Emerald Cat over to Cleo, then hurried over to give the mayor an unwanted shoulder massage.

Back at home, Cleo and her friends found her dad clutching at a pot of ink and adding to the hieroglyphics on the living room wall.

"I thought you were going to try to wash all

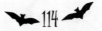

114

that off?" Cleo said.

Niles shook his head. "I rather like it," he said. "It's an exciting adventure story, and much better than anything we get on the magic mirror these days. Nothing but repeats of makeover shows for bog monsters, it seems."

"So, what are you adding to the tale?" asked Luke, peering hard at the freshly painted Egyptian symbols.

"Oh, this?" said Niles. "This is my recipe for rose thorn and nettle soup. It goes very well with a few dried frog skins. In fact, I have a pot bubbling away in the kitchen if you'd all care to join Cleo and me for dinner."

"I'd love to," said Resus, his stomach churning at the thought. "But I've got to dash off for a... You know, it's... Oh, look! Is that Dig outside?"

Chuckling, Luke and Cleo followed Resus out into the street. All three were surprised to see that Dig was indeed outside: the partial pooch was snarling and growling at the Emerald Cat, held tightly in Ramennoodle's arms.

Luke grabbed hold of Dig's collar and struggled to hold him. "It's not a real cat, you dim-witted dog!" he cried.

"Well," said Cleo to the arms. "I guess it's time that you were off. We'll make sure Otto ships your other belongings back to your pyramid without delay."

The arms passed the glimmering green cat statue over to Resus and wrapped themselves around Cleo, giving her a long hug.

"Goodbye, Great-Great-Great-Great-Great-Great-Grandfather Ramennoodle!" she said.

Luke glanced over at Resus. "Don't look at me," said the vampire. "I've stopped counting. Besides, my hands are busy keeping this thing away from Dig!"

One of the arms scurried up Resus's back and over his shoulder to retrieve the Emerald Cat, while the other gave Resus a friendly fist bump, then shook Luke's free hand.

"We might want to hurry up with the goodbyes," said Luke. "I don't think I can hold on to Dig for much longer."

The arms quickly intertwined and, with the Emerald Cat tightly secured, raced off across the street and through the bushes.

Claws scrabbling against the ground, Dig finally managed to break free of Luke's grasp, and, with a joyful bark, the half-dog–half-skeleton gave chase.

"You know," said Luke. "Where I come from, that would be considered a bit weird!"

AN EXCERPT FROM THE
NEW BOOK IN THE SERIES

Chapter One
THE MIRROR

The blood came gushing out, looking red, sticky and delicious. With each life-giving pump of a supposedly long-dead heart, another spurt of the scarlet secretion flowed from the puncture wound and ran down the expanse of pale skin.

"Ow!" cried Alston Negative, pulling the tip of the screwdriver away from where he'd managed to stab himself in the finger. It was always the same. Human tools were made for, well, humans. And he wasn't even vaguely a member of that species.

He was a vampire.

A vampire who was taking down every mirror in the entire house.

Slipping the screwdriver into his pocket, he studied the flow of blood from the cut on his finger. The river of red was almost at his shirt cuff now and, keen as he was to simply stand and watch the life-force continue on its journey, Alston knew he would get into trouble if he caused any extra laundry for his wife.

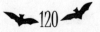 120

So, flicking out a long, pointed tongue, he lapped up the blood.

He'd once been told that drinking your own blood was not good for you; it was simply recycling and not feeding. But that didn't stop the stuff from tasting incredible as it ran down the back of his throat.

"Mmmm," he said to himself. "Just like a well-preserved '67! Yummy!"

"Save some for me!" shouted Bella Negative as she speed-blurred in from the kitchen.

"Oh, I'm sorry!" said Alston. "It has all gone now." He held his clean finger out towards his wife. "But if you want to take a bite and continue from where I left off, I will happily look the other way."

Bella scowled. "Don't tease me, Alston!" she scolded. "You know the rules of Scream Street: any vampire caught drinking blood from another living being will be banished to the Underlands."

Alston sighed. She was, of course, correct. Every vampire household in Scream Street had three taps over their kitchen sink: hot water, cold water and blood. The blood was syphoned out of the wastewater supply in the normal world,

then passed through 13 different types of filtration (mainly to stop scabs getting through and causing naive vampires to choke), then plumbed into the houses.

The result was a bit like a drink labelled as "fruit flavour". All the flavours mingled together. You couldn't single out one specific blood type or taste the individual terror of someone as they held a potentially serious gushing wound over the drain.

Alston sighed. It wasn't like the old days, when you could just transform into a bat and flap out of one of the windows of your castle, bound for the throat of some terrified peasant to get the good stuff right from the source.

But then again, since the Negative family had moved to Scream Street, they hadn't opened the door to an angry mob wielding pitchforks and flaming torches even once. And no one had tried to hammer a wooden stake through his heart while he slept in his coffin.

You had to take the good with the bad.

"I still don't get it," said Bella, dragging her husband from his daytime nightmares. "Do we really have to take down the mirrors every time the

 122

relatives come over?" She held the mirror as Alston slipped a long, sharp fingernail into the head of the screw and used that to complete his task.

"I'm afraid so," he replied. "We don't want to draw attention to Resus's little, er ... problem. Remember last time, when Uncle Vlad spotted that our son had a reflection? I don't think I will ever hear the end of—"

Mr and Mrs Negative froze as they spotted their son's image in the polished surface of the mirror. He must have entered the room while they were chatting. He didn't look happy.

"Ah," said Alston, turning from the reflection to the real thing. "I didn't see you there for a moment."

"I gathered that," said Resus, flatly.

Bella blushed, her cheeks flushing from pure white to off-white. "We didn't mean..."

"Do you think I *like* having a reflection?" Resus barked.

"I'm sorry!" Bella insisted. "We didn't realize you were here..."

"Well, I am," said Resus angrily. "Even if you'd rather I wasn't!"

Alston and Bella could only share an

embarrassed glance as their son stormed out of the house, slamming the front door behind him.

Outside, Resus stomped around to a small flap built into the side of the house and slumped down beside it. Reaching inside his cloak, he pulled out an ancient, rancid chicken leg and placed it on the ground near the flap. Then he produced a can of black hairspray and gave his fringe a quick blast.

Despite being born to vampire parents, Resus was something of a genetic oddity. He had naturally blond hair, wore clip-on fangs and nails, and the mere thought of drinking blood made his stomach churn.

At least his friends didn't care about his lack of freakishness. Not like his parents. Oh, they might *say* they didn't mind hanging around for him to catch up, out of breath, after they had speed-blurred to Eefa's Emporium for tea, but he could always tell that his dad had grown bored while he waited.

More than once, he'd caught him perusing such popular magazines as *Which Witch?* and *Grossmopolitan* while he passed the time. On one occasion, Alston was halfway through a quiz to

"Find the Love Potion To Ensnare the Paranormal Creature of Your Dreams" when Resus had finally arrived.

There was a rusty squeak as the hatch swung open and a disgusting pink leech slimed out into the open air.

"Hello, Lulu! Come on, girl!"

The animal bounded over to him and began to lick the back of his hand with a long, calloused tongue.

"At least someone loves me," said Resus quietly. He tickled the leech under what might have been her chin, then pushed himself to his feet and wandered out through the gate into Scream Street.

Lulu followed at full slither.

Luke Watson gripped the handle of the tennis racket and stared across the row of gravestones at his opponent. On the other side of the graveyard, Cleo Farr hopped nimbly from foot to foot and studied her competitor through the ancient Egyptian bandages that enveloped her face.

"My turn to serve," said the mummy. "Are you ready?"

Luke stood his ground, preparing himself for the oncoming match. "Ready as I'll ever be!"

"OK," said Cleo. "Here we go…"

Tossing the ball high into the air, she whacked it across the tombstones to Luke's half of the court.

Lunging to his left, Luke just managed to catch the ball with the strings of his racket and it ricocheted back towards Cleo.

She returned it with a powerful volley.

Jumping to his right this time, Luke lashed out with his racket and – *spoing!* – managed to send it flying back towards his opponent.

Smash! Cleo returned hard.

Ping! Luke was somehow able to get in the way of the ball.

Whack! The ball was shot back over the stone net at top speed.

Gah! Luke dived as far as he could, arm and racket at full stretch, but missed. He landed on the gravestone divider, half on one side of the makeshift tennis court, half on the other.

"I *think* that's another point to me," said Cleo, wincing.

Luke groaned. "You don't say," he wheezed.

Cleo nodded. "To be fair, I *have* had a bit

126

more time to practise than you. Thousands of years more."

"Who's winning?" asked Resus, as he stepped over the court boundary, closely followed by Lulu.

"Who do you think?" grunted Luke, climbing down from the gravestone.

"Hey, Resus!" said Cleo. "What's up?"

Resus sighed hard. "Oh, you know…"

"What's up?" the mummy asked again.

"Nothing," muttered Resus, spotting the tennis ball at his feet. He tapped it with his toe, sending it rolling over towards Lulu. As it reached the leech, the ball blinked, revealing a hidden eye, then screwed itself shut again. "Apart from being an embarrassment to my whole family, that is."

"Well, I'm not exactly the son my parents wanted, either," Luke pointed out.

"At least your father doesn't hate you," said Resus.

"Your father doesn't hate you," Cleo countered. "He's just embarrassed to have you around sometimes."

Resus blinked.

"I'm not helping, am I?" Cleo asked.

"Not much, no," said Resus, shaking his head.

Luke picked up the tennis ball. "Come on," he said. "I think this is Game Over."

"Yeah," agreed Cleo. "A drink at Eefa's will cheer up Captain Gloom here."

"I doubt it," said Resus. "The way I feel right now, I wish the ground would just open up and swallow me."

The vampire took a step to follow his friends – then got his wish! He fell down, sliding through an opening in the grass and disappearing completely.

"You don't mean that, Resus," said Luke, turning to smile at his friend. But there was no one there.

"Resus?" Luke and Cleo called out together.